MOONSHINER
THE WITNESS

SAM PEMBERTON

Publishing Coordinator – Sharon Kizziah-Holmes

Paperback-Press
an imprint of A & S Publishing
Paperback Press, LLC
Springfield, Missouri

ISBN -13: 978-1-960499-73-8

ACKNOWLEDGEMENTS

As always, special thanks to Sharon Kizziah Holmes, publishing coordinator. I don't know what I'd do without her help and guidance. I don't think any of my books would have been published if I hadn't met this lady.

L. Kennedy, proofreader/editor. This young lady did a wonderful job for me on this book as well as others. Many thanks go to her for her time and efforts to make the book better.

PREFACE

Seth Tabor had a panoramic view from the top of the bluff on the west side of Big Creek. A cornfield immediately below the bluff and Coy Bryant's barn were the closest to him. Making handles for farm tools out of the hickory trees growing on the bench land was how he supported himself.

The day started with him trying to locate a tree to make more handles but when he stopped to check the activities along the creek what he saw changed his life. A shotgun blast followed by another one immediately and the activities following kept his attention the rest of the day.

Curiosity after the shooting led him to a church at Cozy, a community a few miles west from his property. While he was there to find out about what he saw from the bluff, he met the first girl he ever had an interest in getting to know.

After finding out one of the victims of the shooting was her uncle, Seth made a date to sit with her at the funeral.

His relationship with Melissa Bryant changed his life. It evolved into marriage and leaving the place where he witnessed the shooting.

The things he saw from the top of the bluff and the questions he was asked continued to haunt him. A visit from the Searcy County Sheriff and a continual flow of other questions and conversations kept what he saw alive.

How much could he see from over two hundred yards away? And could he identify anyone from that distance? The things he saw and the things he knew were not questions he wanted to answer.

Because of the relationship he developed with Melissa's family or to avoid being part of a murder, he became a reluctant witness. His decision becomes the story of the "Moonshiner, the witness."

CHAPTER 1

Seth Tabor stood looking to the east. He was on the west side of Big Creek, just below the last crossing before it joined the Buffalo River. Seth had moved into the area a few years earlier, after he left railroad construction.

He was in his early twenties. He was just under six feet tall. He had a shock of red hair and several freckles. He was a sturdily built young man. The years he spent driving spikes to secure the rails of the train to the cross ties had built some strong muscles.

He still wore the heavy dungarees and boots from the years when he was constructing the railroad. He had moved to Searcy County, Arkansas and settled on the top of a bluff above the mouth of Big Creek.

The cabin was next to the bluff, with a spring flowing out of a crevice in the rock. While his cabin was beside the water, the cabin was excavated into the bluff and built with three sides, using the bluff as part of his cabin. There was a wood stove for cooking and heat with dirt for the floor. It was comfortable for a man living alone. Seth was looking at the trees growing where the hillside met the bench-land. The dirt was a sandy loam on top of the bluff. The soil was shallow and the hickory trees growing in the area grew slowly and were tight grained. They made excellent handles for farm tools.

Seth had started making handles shortly after he bought the property from Coy Bryant. He owned forty acres that extended to the bottom of the bluff and joined Big Creek. His land was at the top of the bluff and consisted of the bench-land with a hillside beginning above. His cabin was just south of where he was trying to locate the right tree to start making more handles.

Seth was drawn to the area by rumors of a cousin who discovered silver while digging a place to build his cabin, similar to the one Seth built. Rumors was the silver was pure enough that he melted it into bars and was able to sell them. He was a distant cousin on the Tabor side to Seth.

Seth kept to himself and sold the handles to various people in the area, including Willie Sitton, whose barn and blacksmith shop sat at the Big Creek Bridge Crossing, several miles upstream from Seth. Seth had not really become acquainted with anyone other than Coy Bryant, who he recognized on sight because he bought corn from him at the barn in the field below his cabin.

He arrived early to locate the tree for more handles. After cutting the tree and trimming the limbs, he would drag it with his mule to the working area, where it would be shaped into billets prior to making handles. An ax and a buck-saw were the only tools needed for cutting the tree. His dog accompanied him.

He liked to look down at the activity along Big Creek from the top of the bluff. From his vantage point, to the north he could see the water of Big Creek flowing into Buffalo River. The view to the south was blocked by a mountain. Across the creek, he could see where a schoolhouse was under construction. He could see all of the cornfield and the big barn next to the cedar glade.

This morning, he watched the arrival of a buggy as it circled Coy Bryant's barn and parked in the cedar glade above. He didn't realize it was a woman until he saw her enter the barn and disappear. A few minutes later, he watched as Coy Bryant rode his horse around the barn and tied the horse to a tree next to where the buggy was parked. A few minutes later, he saw Coy disappear into the barn after her.

While he was curious about what was happening, Seth returned to his search for the tree. He walked toward a tree he thought would be suitable to make handles. He began cutting the tree, and made sure his dog was not in the area where the tree was going to fall. His concern for the dog interrupted his thoughts of trying to imagine what was going on in the barn. There was only one reason why Coy Bryant would be meeting a woman in the barn.

CHAPTER 2

The noise from the tree falling was not loud enough to interrupt the crows that were on the hill above the barn. They continued making their calls, as they had done all morning. It was quiet for just a few minutes as Seth returned to the edge of the bluff and was watching a wagon crossing the creek, headed toward the barn.

He did not recognize the team of mules or the driver of the wagon. He was watching the wagon when suddenly there was a blast that sounded like a shotgun. Immediately, there was a second blast and then a wild scramble as the mules pulling the wagon turned in a circle, running away from the barn. Seth watched the wagon, and at the same time, he saw a rider come out of the glade above the barn.

He wasn't sure what he saw. He watched the horse and rider as they crossed the field and came west toward Big Creek. The horse disappeared and appeared again as the rider and horse climbed the hill just north of Seth. He did not recognize the rider or the horse. He looked back toward the barn and saw the wagon stop at about where it was before the shotgun blast. The driver of the wagon got off and went into the barn. Seth watched. He had no idea what he had just seen, but while he was wondering what happened, the driver of the wagon returned. The wagon turned around and went back up the creek in the same direction it had come from.

Seth went back to where the tree lay, waiting to be trimmed. He began chopping the smaller limbs until he arrived at the point where he was going to cut the log in lengths for making handles. He left two limbs on opposite sides, about two inches long, to secure the chain when he wrapped it around for dragging. He began to saw and then stopped. Seth returned to the ledge and watched the barn. He thought he could see a wisp of smoke spiraling upward out of the barn. He wondered if it could've been smoke from the shotgun. The crows had gone back to making their usual noise. After standing watching for several minutes, he returned to the log. Then he heard shouting from the direction of the barn.

Seth sat down on a rock and began to watch as a crowd gathered at the barn. It would be over half a mile for him to go around the bluff and climb down and cross the creek to the barn. He decided to just sit and watch.

CHAPTER 3

Seth left the bluff and went to get his mule to drag the log. Seth's mule was a large gray with a light mane. He fed the mule some grain he had purchased from Coy Bryant, along with some cane and other forage growing in the spring water flowing below his cabin. He would divert some of the water into a small vegetable patch. He kept a goat for milk and tethered the goat to a line that he moved continuously, allowing the goat to forage on the underbrush.

He had been to Coy's barn several times to pick up grain. He had an understanding that he was to keep track of the grain and pay for it whenever he saw him. Seth wondered why Coy never came out of the barn while he was watching from the bluff. He tried to remember how many sacks of grain he owed for. He decided it was three, then corrected himself. He always tied the bags of grain across the mule with each bag tied to the other. It had to be four.

He put the harness on the mule and hooked the single tree on one hame and wrapped the log chain around the other. He started leading the mule back to where the log was. He tied the mule to a small bush and decided to go to the edge of the bluff and see if anything else was going on at the barn.

Once again, he sat down on the rock and was startled by how many people were gathered in the barnyard. There was the original wagon and team which arrived before the two-shotgun blasts. Seth paused and tried to count the number of wagons scattered around the hill above the barn, and those in front. There were no loud voices to be heard. He watched as a wagon arrived with two men sitting in the drivers' seat. They stopped a good distance from the barn and did not leave the wagon. He recognized the driver of the first wagon as the one who made a circle before returning after the two shotgun blasts. He was standing with his back to Seth, with two men who appeared to be questioning him. It was some two hundred yards or better from where Seth sat on the rock to the barn. It was too much distance to actually see or hear what was happening.

From looking at the sun and the angle it was striking the tree below the barn, the shadow indicated it was noon or after. Seth could see a man standing in the opening of the hallway into the barn. The man appeared to be holding what had to be a rifle or shotgun across his body.

Seth returned to his mule and hooked the chain around the log to drag it. He led the mule as he dragged the log toward his cabin. While he was trying to return to work, his thoughts continued to imagine what had happened in the barn. As he walked along, leading the mule, he recounted what he had seen. He remembered a couple of other times seeing the buggy parked where it was today, but he had never seen the woman go into the barn before. He had no idea who she was. Also, he had seen Coy ride up and tie his horse to the buggy and go into the barn a couple of times before. Seth began to think about what this all could mean.

He stopped the mule and unhooked the chain from the log. He rolled it over next to the cross stanchions he had built for cutting the log into lengths for each type of handle he planned to make, and where he split the billets. He did not lift the end of the log up onto the blocks. He took the harness off the mule and tethered him to the line where he wanted him to forage for the rest of the day. His curiosity was too great. Seth was going back to sit on the rock and watch what was happening at Coy Bryant's barn.

CHAPTER 4

While Seth was dragging the log and unhooking his mule, the crowd had grown larger. The wagon with the two men was still parked where it was. A tall man sat next to the driver of the wagon. While the driver looked familiar, Seth was not sure he had ever seen the other man before. The driver of the first wagon walked over and started a discussion with the men who remained seated on the last wagon to arrive. Seth noted the similarity of the first wagon and the second one. He tried to remember where he had seen the wagons before.

Seth was trying to guess about what had happened when he saw a buggy arrive with a horse following it. The man riding the horse seemed to be in charge of the situation, and went with the driver of the buggy into the barn. The man who was driving the buggy carried a bag similar to what a doctor always carried. Seth became more curious. He could not imagine what had happened that would require all of this attention, unless the shotgun blast was part of a murder. He waited and watched as the activity shifted to the front of the barn with all the people gathering in front of the man who was guarding the entrance.

Seth leaned forward, trying to see better, but at this distance it made very little difference. He couldn't understand all the people waiting outside the barn and could not visualize what was going on inside. He had been seated for a long time before he saw the driver of the original wagon turn and back the mules and the wagon toward the barn. A few minutes later, three men emerged, carrying what appeared to be a body wrapped in canvas. Seth could not see if it was tied with ropes. They carried out a second body, wrapped exactly as the first. The crowd began to disperse soon after the bodies were loaded into the wagon.

The two men on the second wagon had remained seated during the process of loading what Seth assumed was two bodies. He remembered seeing Coy Bryant go into the barn. He did not see him among the crowd, nor did he seem to be part of what took place after the blasts were heard. Seth assumed he was one of the bodies, and he assumed the woman was the other one. He had come to the ledge to cut the tree a couple of hours after sun up. The shadows from the sun setting behind him were now beginning to cover part of the cornfield. The wagons crossed the creek and went out of Seth's sight. He returned to his cabin. He regretted he had not gone down to the barn, but, as was his nature, he avoided the crowd. His curiosity was increasing as he began to prepare something to eat.

CHAPTER 5

Seth slept late the next morning. The sun was up, and the mule was braying loudly and was being answered by another mule from across Big Creek, where the schoolhouse was being built. Seth watered the mule and looked for the goat. Seth used the goat to supply him with milk, and it also kept the brush down around the cabin. The cabin had a sod roof which extended from the hill out over the cabin. He had spent a great deal of time figuring out how to do the thatch underneath the sod. He did not know how to put the sod on where it would not leak and not grow through the thatch. He went down Buffalo River, to where one of the men who worked with him on the railroad had built a cabin similar to his. When Seth came back and changed the thatch to match his friend's roof, he didn't have any more problems with leaks.

He cut the log into lengths for the handles and split the billets. He started shaping the billets before putting them on the lath. He was having trouble concentrating on his work. He knew there was no need to try to go see Coy Bryant. He was sure he was one of the bodies. He thought back to what he saw immediately after the two blasts. He had seen the mules trying to run away as they pulled the wagon approaching the barn. He had seen a man riding a horse directly toward him. The sun was bright and in Seth's face. It had all happened so fast, he wasn't sure what he saw and in what order. By the time he noticed the horse and the rider, his attention had gone back to the wagon as the driver got the mules under control and went back to the spot in front of the barn. He believed he had heard the water splashing as the horse and rider crossed the creek below him. He then got a glimpse of the horse and rider as they were climbing the hill, they were probably two hundred yards to the north of where he was sitting.

He continued working on the billets as he tried to remember what he saw when the horse and rider were going up the hill. He believed it was a chestnut-colored horse with a black mane. He smiled when he thought how hard it was to recall what he had seen the day before. He remembered hearing people giving a description with a lot of details. Seth doubted that. He had spent the day before observing the field and the barn. He could not remember if the buggy and Coy Bryant's horse were still in the glade above the barn. He decided to go look and see if they were still there.

He enjoyed the walk back to the top of the bluff. He sat down on the rock where he had been sitting the day before and tried to recall more of what he saw. Coy Bryant's horse and the buggy were gone. There was a horse tied to the hitching post in front of the barn. Seth believed it was the horse belonging to the man following the buggy. He had gone into the barn with the man carrying the little bag. From this distance, the bag appeared to be the kind doctors carried. Seth sat for a few minutes, trying to reconcile what he had seen the day before with what he remembered. He left the rock and went back to work on the handles.

CHAPTER 6

The work on the handles was going smoothly, even while Seth was preoccupied with what he had seen at the barn. He was making four ax handles and three hoe handles. Making the hoe handles was easier than making the handles for the axes and more enjoyable. Shaping the billets for the handles did not require him to concentrate but the actual shaping of the handles did. His mind could not move on from what he saw at the barn.

Picking up the last handle from where he was working, he took it to the rack where the finished handles were hanging. There were nine handles ready for delivery, three ax handles and three each of the hoe and sledge hammer handles. It was decided. Seth would harness his mule, a large gray mule perfect for carrying cargo. The mule also was good to ride with a saddle, if he was going any distance. Seth could relax as he rode because the mule was surefooted. Seth liked to ride along the ridges above the cabin.

In a very short time, the mule was saddled and the handles were hanging behind the saddle. He was going to the bridge and see Willie Sitton. Willie always bought the handles even when Seth delivered them without notice. The small number of handles tied behind the saddle was considerably short of the fifteen or twenty usually took each trip. But, this time he wanted to see what Willie knew about the barn and whatever happened there.

The ride was easy. The leaves were beginning to fall, and the trail was mostly covered by them. The mule had no trouble following the trails. Seth arrived at Willie's barn. He sat on the mule and observed the two wagons parked beside the barn. They were the two wagons he had seen after the shotgun blast. While he was sitting observing the wagons, Willie came out of the barn.

"What's going on, Seth?" Willie's voice boomed, and the sound startled Seth.

He was always amazed at how loud and strong Willie's voice was for his size. Willie, at five feet seven inches was at least a head shorter than Seth. Seth observed Willie before he answered.

"Brought a few handles," Seth answered as he dismounted from the mule. He led the mule to the hitching rail and tied him up before Willie responded.

"I can always use whatever handles you bring me, Seth," Willie said as he walked over and shook hands.

Seth hesitated before he stuck out his hand and shook with Willie. He had never shaken hands with Willie before. It was neither one of their styles. They usually did not get close to each other until after they finished their greetings.

This morning was different. Seth could feel the curiosity in Willie's eyes as he had looked at the mule, the handles, and finally, him.

After they shook hands, Willie invited him inside the barn. Seth followed.

"You want another quart of shine as part of your payment?" Willie asked.

Seth thought about how much shine he had left in the quart Willie had given him the last time he brought handles. It had been over two months, and he still had more than half of the quart.

"No, I don't need any, I've still got quite a bit left," Seth finally answered.

Willie did not offer to make them a toddy. He left the toolshed and tack room, and Seth followed him. When he got back to where the mule was tied, he began removing the handles and looking at each one of them.

"These are as good or better than the last ones," Willie commented after he had put the handles next to the anvil in his shop.

Willie sat down on the stool next to the bellows. He pointed to another stool, and Seth sat down without either one commenting.

They sat in silence. Seth was wanting to ask a lot of questions. He had recognized both of

Willie's wagons as being at Coy Bryant's barn. He was quite sure Willie had been on the second wagon when it arrived. The curiosity was making Seth nervous. Finally, Willie broke the silence.

"Your place is on the bluff across Big Creek from Coy Bryant's barn?" Willie finally asked.

"Yeah," Seth answered as he anticipated the next question.

"You didn't come down to the barn yesterday," Willie continued. "Did you see any of that mess?"

Seth thought for a minute. He wasn't sure how to answer. He wasn't going to tell Willie, that he had spent almost all day watching from the bluff across the creek.

"I was too far away to see what was going on." Seth gave out his best answer.

"Somebody killed Coy Bryant and my wife's sister-in-law" Willie added. "With a shotgun."

Seth did not comment.

"It was a mess," Willie used the same words again to describe the happenings. "I sat on my wagon with Preacher Ed, and we didn't get off except to go relieve ourselves in the glade." Willie was struggling to discuss the murders.

Seth finally asked, "What were they doing together? And who would've shot them?"

Willie stood up, motioning for Seth to follow him.

"Come on, let's go to the barn. I'm going to make us a toddy." Willie walked briskly toward the barn. "You could see more from the top of the bluff than anybody could at the barn." Willie made the observation as they entered the tack room and he started to make them a toddy.

Seth sat patiently, waiting for Willie to finish making the toddy. He was cautious about what he should say after he learned the woman was Willie's sister-in-law. Seth came from Kentucky, and he knew several people with stories of people who got shot for messing around with someone else's wife. He looked down at a knothole in the floor. He was studying the knothole, trying to figure out how much he knew and how much he should say.

Finally, he answered. "I was looking for a tree to cut and make handles when I saw the woman in the buggy park and go into the barn," Seth said. After Willie handed him the toddy, he took a couple of sips and then added, "Not long after she went into the barn, Coy Bryant tied his horse up next to the buggy and followed her."

Seth paused and then added, "I recognized Coy Bryant because I bought my land from him, and I still buy corn from him at the barn."

Seth stopped with the description of what he saw. He did not mention seeing the horse and rider coming toward him across the cornfield. He also did not mention hearing the water splashing as the horse crossed Big Creek. He wasn't sure how well he saw the horse and rider while they were climbing the hill. He sat, thinking about what he had seen, while Willie was sipping his toddy and observing him.

Willie Sitton was sure Seth Tabor was not telling him everything he had seen. Willie did not go into any details about sister Rhodes, Willie's wife's sister-in-law who was shot in the nude with Coy Bryant. He figured Seth knew Ellen's brother Jim Rhodes, who operated the store in Big Flat. He didn't know Seth well enough to have an open discussion, and didn't want to give any impression about how he felt toward Coy Bryant.

They finished drinking their toddy and sat in silence until Willie asked how much money he owed for the handles. Seth left the barn with twenty dollars and a jar of honey. He liked Willie Sitton, and he was sorry to learn there was any connection between him and the incident in the barn.

CHAPTER 7

The ride back from Willie's barn had been easy. Seth sat on the mule and allowed him to travel at his own pace while he thought about how little he had learned about the murders. He only knew the identity of the people killed. He had heard of the woman referred to as Sister Rhodes. He knew her husband, Jim Rhodes, was active in the church at Cozy, and he was a respected storekeeper. He knew Coy Bryant was the area's biggest farmer and also very active in the church at cozy.

Seth got back to his cabin and did his usual chores. He fed the mule from the grain he had not paid for. He wondered whom he needed to pay since the man he owed was dead. He decided to watch the barn and see who became the new owner, or who would be making an investigation of the murders.

He worked on the handles he was making from the tree he had cut two days before. His mind was still preoccupied with what he had seen and was continually trying to sort through the memory.

He decided what he saw was a meeting between Coy Bryant and a woman who was his lover. He decided he had gotten a glimpse of the man who fired the shot. He wondered if he would recognize the rider of the horse. Seth decided he wouldn't be able to identify him. But he knew he could identify the horse.

He worked on the handles until they were finished a couple of days later. Seth had trouble keeping his days straight, and wasn't sure if the next day was Sunday. He decided to walk to Cozy, and if it was Sunday, he would go to church. If it wasn't, he would go and see the man he bought the goat from. He was curious what the gossip would be when he got to Cozy.

Seth arrived at the church at Cozy. It obviously was Sunday. His eyes followed the crowd assembled in front of the church. He had gotten there early. The women and children were standing close to the steps. Most of the men were huddled around either one of the wagons or standing next to their horses. He recognized the Avey man whom he had bought the goat from. Seth walked up and didn't say anything until Carl Avey turned and spoke to him. When he asked what Seth was doing at church, it startled Seth.

Before he could answer, Carl said," There's been a lot happening, and I guess you're like the rest of the crowd: wondering about what's going to happen to the church since Coy Bryant was killed with another man's wife."

Seth blushed. "I just..." he paused and could not continue. He didn't have a good explanation of why he was at a church he'd only been to twice in four years—once when his friend from the railroad got married, and another time when one of the buyers of his handles died and they had a funeral.

The crowd started to go into the building, but Carl and the two men he was visiting with stayed outside.

"Who do you think will replace Coy Bryant as Sunday school superintendent?" one of the men standing next to Carl asked.

Seth had never seen him before, and he had no idea about the responsibilities of a Sunday school superintendent.

"Fred Hudson," Carl answered.

Seth followed the men into the building and sat down on the back pew, next to the man who had asked about Coy Bryant's replacement.

CHAPTER 8

Seth met a young lady after church. He found her very attractive and was able to start a conversation.

She said, "I have never seen you before."

Seth was a little tongue-tied as he admired her beautiful red hair. It was almost the same color as his.

"Me neither," he answered. He meant to say, "I've never seen you before, either,"

Seth got over being tongue-tied and found out her name was Melissa Bryant. She did not tell him her relationship to Coy Bryant.

Another relative came up and interrupted them. She said, "Uncle Coy's funeral is Wednesday."

Seth felt a little bit embarrassed about trying to get acquainted with a girl after attending church under the circumstances. But he continued to visit and eventually Melissa agreed for him to come and sit with her at the funeral.

Seth walked home. His mind was totally confused. He had gone to Cozy to learn gossip. The only thing he had learned was that one of the victims of the shooting was going to be buried in the Rock Creek Cemetery on Wednesday. He got home and changed into his work dungarees. He fed the mule. He milked the goat and harvested the last of the pumpkins from the garden.

Monday morning was colder than usual. The sun had not broken through the layer of clouds. They were hanging low, like it could turn much colder and bring a snow. Seth finished his chores early and was walking toward the bluff to take a look at the barn. He saw the horse and rider who came the day of the murder. He watched the horse and rider come across the cornfield toward the crossing of Big Creek, just north of his property. Seth continued to watch the barn, and there didn't appear to be anyone else around it.

He had turned back toward his cabin when he heard the horse approaching from behind. He turned and realized it was the sheriff. Seth had seen Sheriff Joe Carson a few times, Whenever he was delivering handles to the hardware store in Marshall. The sheriff was always riding the same horse he was riding today.

Seth stood still while Joe rode up and dismounted. Joe Carson introduced himself.

"I am the sheriff of Searcy County. Joe Carson," He paused before sticking out his hand.

Seth shook it.

Joe turned and started walking toward the edge of the bluff. He stopped by the rock where Seth had sat watching the day of the murder.

"You could see a lot from here," Joe commented. "But you were too far a way to see any details."

"Do you know which County Coy Bryant's barn is located in?" He pointed toward the barn.

"It may be in Marion County," Joe said. "I know the county line comes through somewhere along here."

Seth followed and stood alongside Joe as he was looking at the barn. He waited to see if there was going to be more questions.

"I was by Willie Sitton's place yesterday," the sheriff continued, turning to face Seth with a questioning stare. Seth looked away without making a comment. He looked toward the barn avoiding the questioning look.

CHAPTER 9

The sheriff sat down on the end of a rock. He was looking at the cornfield and the barn some two hundred yards below the top of the bluff. Seth sat down on the opposite end of the rock. They both sat quietly for several minutes.

"You could see everything?" Joe asked Seth.

"Yeah," Seth answered pausing again before he added, "I could see horses and wagons, but I could not see what the people were doing."

"What was going on when you heard the first shot?" the sheriff asked.

"The mules and wagon had just crossed the creek and were getting close to the barn," Seth answered.

"What happened next?"

Seth paused and thought for a minute. He wasn't sure where the mules were when the first shot was fired. He finally answered, "The mules got spooked by the shotgun blast and were trying to run back the way they had come. I was watching that, I guess when the second blast happened," Seth had been continuously going over what he had seen for over a week now.

Sheriff Joe Carson was studying the barn, the glade above it, and the road from the creek crossing to the barn. He was trying to visualize what Seth had seen.

"You see the rider and the horse leave the barn?" he asked.

Again, Seth tried to remember what he had seen and the order in which he had seen it.

"When I saw the rider, I think he had just come out of the glade and headed toward me across the cornfield," Seth answered.

The sheriff was not looking at him. He was looking at the cedar glade above the barn and trying to figure out how long it took the shooter to leave the barn and get on his horse. He wondered how he left the barn. He knew he didn't come out toward the mules and the wagon.

The driver of the wagon had gotten turned around and had come back toward the barn very quickly. Seth had told the sheriff he got a glance of the rider as he went over the small ridge into the cornfield heading west. The sheriff wondered how he was able to get on his horse that quickly after the blast.

He had spent several minutes observing the field and trying to imagine what Seth could've seen.

He finally asked, "Could you tell anything about the rider and the horse?"

Seth stood up from the rock and took a couple of steps forward to the north as he tried to remember the horse and the rider as he came into the cornfield.

"I could not see them real good, the sun was shining bright with a glare. I don't think I could see them well enough to give a description while they were in the cornfield." Seth wished he had not started answering questions.

He stood up on the rock, and the sheriff remained seated on the other end. Seth was trying to decide how many more questions he was going to try to answer. He did not want to become a witness about something which he couldn't really say for sure what he had seen.

"You couldn't see the horse cross the creek," the sheriff commented as a matter of fact while he was looking toward the creek below.

The conversation ended for a while, and Seth sat back down on the rock. Sheriff Joe Carson stood up on the rock and looked toward the hill north of Seth's place. He couldn't see very much of the trail that he knew the horse and rider used after they crossed Big Creek.

"You see the horse as it climbed the trail?" Sheriff Carson pointed toward the hill. "You couldn't have told anything about it through these trees," he added, without giving Seth time to answer, and sat back down.

Seth sat quietly waiting for the sheriff to continue. He didn't. Seth didn't tell him that if he went to the edge of the bluff thirty yards to the north, where he had gone after he heard the splashing in the creek from the horse crossing, he would be able to get a better look at the trail going up the hill. He did not volunteer where he was or what he saw because he had no idea who was riding the chestnut-colored horse with the black mane. He knew he would recognize the horse if he ever saw it again.

Sheriff Carson left the ledge, and Seth went back to work on some more handles. His thoughts returned to going to the funeral for Coy Bryant. His only reason for going was to see Coy's niece, Melissa Bryant.

CHAPTER 10

It had been six weeks since Seth went to the funeral. He had gone to see Melissa at least once a week. He had been in church at Cozy more times during that period than ever before in his life.

He had ridden his mule to see her, and they had taken her dad's buggy and gone to Marshall for the day. They tied the buggy next to the spring after allowing the horse to drink out of the trough. He and Melissa walked over to the watering trough and were leaning and looking at the reflection in the water.

Seth loved Melissa's appearance. She was a little over five feet tall, with hair a deeper red than his; their eyes were a matching blue. Melissa's eyes were the only other eyes Seth had ever seen the same color as his. During the last few weeks his feelings had grown intense for her. She was a well-rounded but not a very large young woman. Her freckles were much smaller than his, and color of the freckles blended very well with her smooth skin.

They stood silently, looking at the reflection in the water. Seth gave her a hug when they stood up. He held her hand as they began the walk toward the Searcy County court square. He intended to propose to Melissa by the time they made it to the courthouse. They had never discussed having a life together, and Seth hoped she shared his feelings.

Suddenly, they were standing in the county clerk's office and waiting as the clerk filled out their marriage license. Seth's mind was scrambled. He couldn't actually remember what he had said to Melissa about getting the marriage license. He wasn't sure she even answered. He remembered taking her hand and leading her into the county clerk's office.

They left Marshall and started back to Melissa's house. Her dad's farm was located on a creek just north of Cozy. They made plans for their wedding as they drove home in the buggy. Seth had taken Melissa to his cabin a couple of times. They would not be living on the ledge above her uncle's barn. During the time he was seeing Melissa, he had never mentioned what he saw. But when he had taken her to visit his cabin, they had gone to the rock where he had sat the day it happened.

Melissa sat on the rock and was quiet as she observed the cornfield and barn. She never asked

Seth if he had seen anything. As Seth walked away from the edge of the bluff, he made a decision that this would be Melissa's last trip to his cabin.

He made an offer on a farm between Cedar Creek on Buffalo River and Maumee. He hoped he could close the deal before the wedding. He told Melissa she would not be living in a sod-covered cabin with a dirt floor. He never explained he was bothered by all the gossip and the details he had heard about the murders. He promised himself he would avoid ever being a witness.

CHAPTER 11

Melissa and Seth's wedding was two months after they got the marriage license. He sold the forty acres with the cabin to a fellow named Brown, who was a bachelor and also made handles for farm tools. Seth left all the tools and the handles he was working on with the property.

He sold the mule and the goat, also. There was not much to move when Melissa and Seth moved into their farmhouse. He spent the first two months making repairs to the house and the barn. Melissa's family had overwhelmed them with gifts after the wedding.

Seth was feeding the cows and calves. They had seven cows and three calves. They were all gifts from somebody in Melissa's family. They were generous people. Seth was introduced to all of them, except for one uncle that left for Oklahoma the week of Coy's funeral. He lived closer to St. Joe, in the northern part of Searcy County. His family was running the farm while he went to work at a construction job somewhere in Western Oklahoma.

Seth was inspecting the hinges on the corral gate. He thought about the hinges Fred Hudson had shown him on his corral gate. He liked those hinges because you could pick the gate up and move it without having to take the hinges apart. He liked the way the strap to the gate post had the three-quarter-inch rod which inserted into the gate portion of the hinge. He decided he was going to get a set of those.

Fred told him he bought the hinges at the store in Big Flat. He also told him it was Jim Rhodes' store, whose wife was killed with Coy Bryant.

He decided to go to Big Flat and get some hinges. "Melissa, do you want to ride to Big Flat with me?" He asked her when he was almost ready to go.

"You will have to give me time to get ready," she answered.

After about forty-five minutes, they were in the buggy and on their way. Seth had no idea how long it would take. He had been to Big Flat, but he had crossed Big Creek and rode his mule up the trail through a crevice in the bluff. The wagon trail would follow Turkey Pen Branch Road to Big Creek and would then follow Spring Creek until the road went up the hill to the west side of Big Flat.

They had made good time. In the early 1930s,

Big Flat was a thriving community. It was easy to locate the rock building housing Rhodes' General Merchandise.

"You should get your hair cut while we are here," Melissa said, Then added, "I think Preacher Ed still cuts hair in the front of the store."

Seth did not answer her. He was tying the horse to the hitching rail and making sure he had gotten the buggy out of the street. Melissa left. She was walking toward a dress shop across the street away from the general store.

Seth went into the store and looked for the hardware section where he located the hinges for the corral gate. Everyone was busy. He saw the barber's chair in the front left corner of the store, and there was a group of men waiting for a haircut. He first decided he was not going to wait. Then he thought there was no way to predict how long it would take Melissa in the dress shop. He sat down in one of the chairs to wait his turn for a haircut.

He recognized Paul Avey as the man sitting in the chair. He was the man who had sold him his farm. They did not interrupt their conversation until after Seth was seated.

"Seth, what are you doing in Big Flat?" Paul asked.

The preacher, Ed Tice, stopped cutting hair and looked at Seth.

"This is Seth Tabor, the man who bought my farm," Paul said, and turned his head to look at the preacher. "You know Preacher Ed Tice?" he asked directing his comment to Seth.

"I should, he's the one that got me and Melissa hitched," Seth said.

Everyone in the area of the barber chair laughed at the comment. The conversation resumed after Seth was introduced. He looked around the group of men and realized he only recognized one other person, Fred Hudson, besides Paul and the preacher. He sat quietly and listened, as they were still discussing the shooting on Big Creek after several months.

When Seth left the barber chair after getting his hair cut, he had learned a lot. There was no mention of where he was living at the time of the shooting. He learned the owner of the store had been a suspect. Jim Rhodes was accused of shooting his wife. His alibi was that he had been in Sylamore picking up supplies. The railroad agent gave a copy of the date and time to Sheriff Joe Carson. Jim Rhodes' horse was a light buckskin color with a black mane. The witness driving the wagon for Willie Sitton could not describe the horse or the rider well enough to give a positive identification. According to the barbershop gossip, he had only gotten a glimpse of the rider and the horse after he got control of the mules and his wagon.

There was a lot of discussion about the bodies in the barn. Seth listened as everyone gave a version of both the position of the bodies and where their body was shot. He sat quietly and got his hair cut while all of the discussions went on. He had never told Melissa or anyone how well he had seen the chestnut-colored horse with the black mane as it climbed the hill.

He paid for the hinges and started walking toward the dress shop. He met Melissa.

"We'll have to come back in three weeks and pick up my dress," she said as they met. "Actually, I should have said 'dresses'."

They got into the buggy and turned around, starting toward Cozy. Seth did not ask her how much the dresses cost. He was amazed at how much money Melissa had brought into their marriage. Early on, he was worried about how well he could support her. He worried now that she was too independent and didn't need any of his support.

He liked the smooth ride of the buggy on the sandy portion of the road leaving Big Flat. The horse was traveling at a fast walk, almost a canter. It was an easy trip home. He put the buggy in the shed. He curried the horse and fed him grain. He took the hinges to the gate and measured them to make sure they were what he wanted. They were perfect. It was a good trip, and he would take a few days to consider what he heard during the haircut about the shootings. There were more descriptions than he thought possible, based on what he had seen.

CHAPTER 12

◇◇◇

Seth was finished with installing the new hinges on the corral gate. He had opened and closed the gates several times, and they worked perfectly. He had predrilled pilot holes for the lag screws before he installed the hinges. He couldn't remember where he learned to do that, probably when he was a boy on his family farm in Kentucky.

He thought he remembered learning it from his dad. "son, if we don't predrill the holes for the lag bolts, the movement of the hinges will eventually split the wood". He remembered the sound of his dad's voice. Some days he regretted ever leaving home and going to work on the railroad construction. Today was one of those days. Seth was married. He was happy with Melissa, but he was bothered by all the gossip about the murders he had witnessed.

His thoughts had been consumed by the memories since the day of the shooting, trying to resolve what he knew, what he had seen and what he had heard from other people. While he was standing, admiring his work, he was having the same thoughts again. He listened; he thought he heard the sound of a horse's hooves and the click of buggy wheels in the gravel coming down the road.

He recognized Fred Hudson. He liked Fred, and he liked him even better when he learned Melissa's mother and Fred were cousins. It seemed everywhere Seth was, Fred would eventually show up, or was already there.

Seth replaced the tools he'd been using on the rack above the work bench while the buggy came closer. He hurried out of the shop to meet Fred.

"Where you started?" The question boomed from Seth. He said it louder than he intended, as he had started to speak during the noise from the horse and buggy, but when he actually said it, they had stopped.

Fred didn't answer. He got out of the buggy and went over to inspect the gates to the corral. He admired how evenly the two gates met in the middle when they were closed. He liked the fact the top edges met perfectly in the middle and hung evenly. He opened the left one and swung it toward him, then closed it. Seth stood, watching.

"Those hinges worked perfectly, and you've done a great job installing them, Seth," Fred smiled when he paid Seth the compliment.

They stood admiring the hinges and discussed things about their farms before Fred asked Seth a question.

"What did you think of Preacher Ed, while he was cutting your hair?" Fred asked.

Seth walked over and hooked his arms over the corral fence. He wasn't sure how to answer the question. Was it a question about the quality of his haircut, or was it a question about Preacher Ed's personality? Seth didn't ask for an explanation.

"I like him as a preacher, and he did a good job cutting my hair," Seth answered.

"Red hair is not as easy to cut as other colors," Fred commented, and pulled his hat off, exposing a balding head which still had a good amount of deeper colored red hair than Seth. "Sheriff Joe Carson came to see you right after the shooting?"

The question from Fred surprised Seth. He turned and stood up straight, leaving one elbow resting on top of the corral fence before he answered.

"Yes, he came to my place on the ledge," Seth replied.

"He told me he questioned you about what you saw when he came and talked to me about who I thought it was who did the shooting." Fred was talking smoothly, without any emotion. "Sheriff Joe said he looked off at the field and barn from your bluff, and he doesn't think you were close enough to know anything about what happened."

Fred walked back toward where his horse was tied next to the barn. He untangled the horse's front leg from the bridle rein which had come untied. The horse was standing still, but somehow managed to wrap the reins around its right front leg. Fred retied the reins and turned back, facing Seth.

"Have you heard about people accusing Jim Rhodes of killing his wife and Coy Bryant?" Fred asked.

"I've heard that," Seth answered.

"That boy who works for Willie Sitton, Carl Harris, did not see either the horse or the rider well enough to give a description." Fred paused and then added, "Joe told me, Carl only got a glance of the horse as it disappeared into the cornfield."

He went on to tell Seth all the things he had heard from everyone, and he ended his discussion by saying he doubted anyone would ever be arrested for the murders.

He then paused and asked, "Can a man in Arkansas shoot somebody for messing with his wife?"

Seth had no idea what the answer would be to that question.

They spent the rest of the time visiting about the church at Cozy. Seth realized how much Fred Hudson thought of Preacher Ed Tice. He didn't share any details about the rumors concerning the preacher's drinking. He told Seth about the close friendship between Willie Sitton, the moonshiner and Preacher Ed Tice. He went on to describe how much good Willie Sitton did in spite of him making and selling moonshine whiskey.

"There's not a house in a twenty-five mile radius that doesn't have enough of Willie 'shine to make a poultice or a toddy," Fred ended the discussion.

As he left on his buggy, Seth watched him drive away. He thought how much Fred, the preacher, and Willie Sitton had influenced his life since he settled on the ledge above Big Creek. Willie was one of his best customers for his handles. He met Melissa because he knew there would be a lot of people at Cozy to hear the preacher after the murders. He remembered Willy's story about the sermon Preacher Ed preached following his intoxication.

Seth remembered the glaze in Willie's eyes when he told the story about the sermon. Seth was not there. Seth gained respect for Willie after listening to the story and since he met Melissa, he gained equal respect for Preacher Ed. Seth was becoming part of the community. He went back to the toolshed and began thinking about what his next project would be.

CHAPTER 13

Seth spent the better part of the next day removing handles from tools he needed sharpened. He had been careful not to damage the handles so he could use them again after the tools were sharpened. He decided that the next morning, he was going to take the tools to Willie Sitton. On one of his trips to deliver handles, he watched as Willie finished creating the point on a plow and sharpened a hoe. He needed both things done.

Seth decided he was going to ride Melissa's horse to Willie's blacksmith shop. The shop was next to the big barn at the Big Creek bridge. He started a search for Melissa after he decided he wanted to take her horse. Seth never owned a saddle horse. He liked to ride Melissa's horse but he had always asked her if he could ride it. It was a warm day in mid-February, and the ride to Willie's would be pleasant.

He found Melissa in the back room working on

a quilt. He was amazed at how she was always working to create more things for the house. Seth didn't remember his mother doing all those things.

"Can I ride the horse to Willie's?" Seth asked as soon as she looked at him.

"Why are you going to Willie Sitton's?" she replied.

Seth wondered about the question. She seldom asked why he was doing anything.

"I am taking some tools for him to sharpen in his shop," he answered.

Seth was riding the horse at an easy gate as he got to the ridge and started toward Cozy. The tools rattling and bouncing inside the feed sack was bothering the horse. Seth stopped and rearranged the tools in the sack and tied them across the back of the saddle. When he remounted, the problem was solved. They were not clanging together or bouncing around hitting the horse in the flank. It was a lot better not having to worry about the horse running away because of the tools.

Seth began thinking about all the things happening since the end of October when he watched the murders. A lot of things about his life had changed since then. He went to church at Cozy because he was curious. He had met Melissa there.

He never actually had a girlfriend before Melissa. He was sensitive about his red hair and freckles. People teased him about the color of his hair all the time. He had a couple of scars on his face as a result. One above his left eye, and another one underneath his right jaw, just below his ear. He got both of those when his temper flared after being teased.

He was not selfish and he was not bashful. He just never developed the social skills to talk to a girl. Now that he was married to Melissa, he looked back at the day he first saw her. The surge of attraction he felt for her when he saw her red hair grew even stronger when he saw the matching blue of her eyes. There were several people who commented to them about their hair, their eyes and their skin colors. Seth imagined people were fascinated with a couple looking so much alike.

Time had passed quickly on the one hand, while it seemed to drag on the other. Seth and Melissa's lives just fell into place. Seth was beginning to lose patience with all the questions about what he saw the day of the murders. He wondered if he was becoming paranoid. It seemed wherever he went he was facing questions.

"And you heard the shots, and you saw the people at Coy's barn?" Were the typical questions.

He thought about what he learned about the shooting and the people at the barn. Carl Harris, who worked for Willie, was the first person there. He was driving the mules that turned and ran back with the wagon. He went into the barn and saw the bodies. Seth thought about the different descriptions he heard about the injuries to the bodies. He had listened to a couple of theories from people who believed the woman was not intended to be a victim of the shooting. He heard one man argue, "She was shot so she could not be a witness."

He was anxious to see Willie. He knew now that Willie was the center of information for the area. The people who went to Willie's to buy 'shine always had a story.

"I was there at Willie's barn, when I heard---------" was the usual start for most gossip.

Seth's opinion had changed since the day he sat on the rock watching the barn. He took the facts he knew for sure. He saw a woman go into the barn. He did not recognize her and he didn't think he'd ever seen Jim Rhodes' wife before that day. He watched Coy Bryant tie up his horse next to the buggy and go into the barn. He saw Carl Harris, he'd learned his name later, crossing the creek and driving up to the barn. He heard the shots. All the rest of the activity that day didn't matter except for the horse and rider he watched across the cornfield, heard splashing water as the horse crossed the creek and saw them again climbing the hill north of the ledge.

Seth was sure he was never sharing that information in that order. He was trying to avoid becoming a witness. When he met Melissa, he had no idea it was her uncle until he decided he wanted to be with her. He thought how unusual it was for the circumstances to bring them together.

As he rode the horse along the ridges, headed to Willie's barn, his thoughts continued. He would not be married to Melissa and he would not be riding her horse with tools to be sharpened by Willie Sitton, if the murders had not happened.

CHAPTER 14

The wind had picked up. It was more than a breeze blowing from the south. The leaves had fallen over two months ago. The warmth of the breeze and the sunshine was the first signs Seth had felt of the coming spring. He hoped Willie could get the tools sharpened and he could get them back on their handles in time to plant potatoes.

Melissa had helped him to clean the dead weeds and grass off the garden spot. He added all the manure from the barn for fertilizer. Paul Avey had not cleaned the stables in years. Seth was actually proud. It furnished a lot of good fertilizer for the area they planned to make their first garden.

Seth was coming down the last hill before he reached Willie Sitton's barn. He hoped Willie would be there. He knew Willie was probably there when he saw a buggy, and another wagon sitting beside the buggy.

Seth rode his horse between the buggy and the

wagon. He dismounted and tied his horse to the hitching rail. He looked around for Willie. There was nobody to be seen. He heard laughter coming from the tack room. Seth knocked on the door before he entered.

"Come in, nobody ever knocks around here." Seth recognized Willie's voice.

He entered the little room next to the tack room where five people were sitting around a large block of wood, cut off from a log that made a table for a poker game. All the men turned and looked at him. Seth only recognized Willie. They picked up their cards and held them close to their vest while Willie introduced them to Seth. Seth was too busy observing the room to remember their names. He leaned against the wall in the corner. They asked him to join the game.

"I don't play poker," Seth answered.

"Why?" The player sitting closest to where Seth was standing asked.

"I tried it a couple times and when I won, I didn't like taking other people's money, and when I lost, I didn't like leaving my money in somebody else's pocket," Seth's answer was solemn and serious. It brought a round of laughter from all the people seated at the poker table except Willie.

"You in a hurry, Seth?" Willie asked.

All eyes turned to Seth waiting on his answer. They then looked back at Willie.

"No, not really." Seth looked directly at Willie before adding. "I've just brought some tools for you to sharpen."

"You go ahead and unload the tools in the shop," Willie said. "This game's about over; these boys are running out of money." Willie finished the comment and laughed loudly. None of the other players at the table joined him in his laughter.

Seth started out the door.

"Tie a string to each tool, look in the bin, use a color of string different from the tools in the bin." Willie was talking as he dealt the next hand of cards. "Write your name on the board and the color of string used to mark your tools"

Willie had finished dealing the cards while he was giving Seth instructions. Seth went to his horse and got the sack with the tools.

It took him quite a bit of time to mark each tool by tying the string through the handle hole. Seth looked at the board, he found the piece of chalk for writing his name laying on the ground beneath it. His name was the third name on the board, and his color was a blue string. As he was writing his name, he wondered if Willie would get the tools sharpened by the time, he needed them. The bin holding tools waiting to be sharpened was almost full.

Seth was not going back to where the card game was. He was thinking about walking across the bridge while he waited for Willie to come out. He started to leave the shop when he saw one of the players coming out of the barn carrying two quarts of 'shine. He sat down in the shop and waited for the players to leave. They all left with some of Willie's 'shine.

Willie walked into the blacksmith shop. He was stuffing some dollar bills into the bib pocket of his overalls. Seth couldn't help but stare. He did not mention the money. Willie didn't either.

Willie looked at the board where Seth had written his name and turned to look in the bin at the tools.

"You're going to need them tools to make a garden," Willie observed while he was picking up one of the smaller hoes.

Seth didn't answer, he just nodded his head.

"I'll get them done," Willie stated, with a tone showing he was determined to have them back to Seth before planting season.

"How long you going to stay today?" Willie asked. "I need to feed some steers up the creek."

"I'd like to get home before dark," Seth answered.

Willie opened the big door on the side of the barn where a team of mules stood hooked to a wagon already loaded with feed.

"I was loaded up to go when them fellers got here," Willie said as he walked around the mules and climbed on the wagon. "I plum forgot they were coming to play poker this morning". Seth had followed him to the wagon and gotten on beside him without ever agreeing to go. Seth wondered how Willie managed to attract people. He had found himself doing everything Willie suggested every time he saw him. Today was no different; they were on their way to feed the steers.

CHAPTER 15

Willie stood up on the wagon seat and began calling the steers. Seth sat on the seat, trying to remember how many gates he had opened and closed during the trip to the field where the steers were. He knew they crossed the creek three times. He believed he had opened and closed four gates.

Seth heard the steers running before he saw the first one come over the ridge.

"Seth, help me throw this hay out!!" Willie said with some excitement. "They'll run into the wagon if we don't get some on the ground."

Seth began untying the wire around the bales of hay and was tossing them as far as he could away from the back of the wagon. It took a few minutes to get the hay scattered for the steers. Willie was counting the steers.

"I didn't bring the dog, and we are missing two steers." Willie sat down on the seat and said,

"We'll wait a little while, they may come."

The weather was warmer than it had been earlier during Seth's ride from Cozy. It was comfortable sitting in the sun and watching the steers feed on the hay.

"You're getting acquainted with Preacher Ed?" The way Willie said it made it a question.

Seth thought for a minute before he answered. The first time he heard Preacher Ed Tice preach was at Coy Bryant's funeral. He had gone to church several times just to see Melissa, and hated to admit he spent more time thinking about her during the sermons than listening to the preacher. But before he answered Willie, he realized he was learning a lot about Preacher Ed Tice.

"Yeah, I like the man," Seth answered as he remembered the day, he spent at Big Flat getting his hair cut. He wondered how close Willie was to the preacher. He had heard the stories about the preacher getting drunk with Willie.

"Preacher Ed rides with me, just like you are, to feed my cows," Willie explained. "He wants to drive the mules; he got tired of opening gates."

Seth appreciated that comment. He dreaded opening the gates on the return trip to the barn. Willie handed him the reins to the team of mules. He would get to drive the wagon back to the barn.

"Preacher Ed has worried a lot about the murders," Willie stated without knowing what he was going to say next. "Melissa is Coy Bryant's niece." Willie began a review of Melissa's family. He told

Seth about her dad and his brothers. "Melissa's dad is a hard worker and a good man." He paused. "There is a reason Coy got shot."

They finished the conversation while the steers were eating the hay, and Seth was driving the mules as they started back to the barn. Most of their conversation was about Preacher Ed. Willie was very complimentary of the preacher. Seth realized Willie was not going to reveal anything bad, if he knew it, about Preacher Ed. He explained how much he and the preacher appreciated their friendship. After Willie made the comment about there being a reason Coy was shot, he didn't mention Jim Rhodes's wife.

They got back to the barn. Seth watered Melissa's horse from the watering tank beside the barn. He wondered where the pipe bringing the water to the tank came from. Willie unharnessed the mules and turned them loose in the lot. They immediately wallowed in the dirt.

"That's the reason I don't brush them down anymore," Willie said to Seth as they watched the mules rolled over in the dirt. Willie insisted Seth take Melissa some of the molasses he had stored in the tack room. Seth left the barn after spending a good day with Willie. He listened to Willie's description of Melissa's family. He had heard enough gossip to know what Willie meant about Coy getting shot. He knew Haskell Bryant, his father-in-law, was a good man. He couldn't believe how much he had done for him since he married Melissa.

The horse was rested and made good speed on the trip home. He didn't know how much of a report he would give Melissa about his day with Willie Sitton.

CHAPTER 16

Seth listened to the little brown mule as he was chewing the corn. Fred Hudson seemed to be able to fill every need Seth and Melissa came up with. Evidently, he was at Willie's barn a couple of days after Seth dropped the tools off to be sharpened.

He came by and asked, "Where are you going to make the garden?"

Seth and Melissa took him on a tour below the barn where they expanded the garden spot. Seth had completed the web wire fence for the new boundary of the garden.

He came back two days later, leading a mule with a full set of harnesses. The harness was in great shape. and the mule wouldn't weigh over five hundred fifty pounds. He was about half the size of the mule Seth sold with his forty acres.

"I sold this mule to one of the Baker boys," Fred said after he led the mule into the yard. "He's going to California. I gave him ten dollars and bought the mule and harness back."

Fred handed the reins to Seth. "Just consider it a late wedding gift," he added.

Seth and Melissa both objected to him giving them the mule. Melissa had a full set of silverware the Hudson's brought after they moved into the house. She didn't know if Fred knew his wife gave her the silverware. She did not mention it.

Seth led the mule to the barn, removed the harness, and dumped the corn into the feeding bin. It was settled.

Seth retrieved a plow from the storage area of the toolshed. He inspected the plow. It was a double-shovel. It would be perfect for breaking the garden and planting the potatoes. He wished he had taken the plow points to Willie for sharpening. He decided he would find out soon enough if they would work. He couldn't wait to see if the little mule could pull the plow.

Seth gave the mule extra corn. He left the barn after feeding the mule to admire the work they had done in the new garden plot. He had plowed in three directions. He first plowed across the width and then he had plowed twice at two different angles of the full-length of the garden. It was not as rocky as he expected.

Seth was having to reach back into his memories to when he was growing up in the mountains of Eastern Kentucky. He couldn't say if he ever remembered actually breaking ground for a garden before. He knew he plowed corn using a double-shovel, but he never did break ground with one. There was not a turning plow in the toolshed. He was pleased with the work and with the mule. He laughed when he thought of the old saying "don't look a gift horse in the mouth". He remembered his grandfather telling him that meant not to check the horse's age. Seth had no idea what to look for if he looked in a horse's mouth and he didn't know if it worked the same in mules.

Melissa did not come out of the house while Seth was plowing in the garden. He didn't know she was visiting with a neighbor until he went in for supper.

"Ethel Hayes came by," Melissa said as she set the plates on the table.

"Was anyone with her?" Seth asked. The Hayes family lived less than a mile up the hollow from Seth and Melissa's farm.

"No, they went to Big Flat and she came to tell me the buttons for my dresses did not come in," Melissa answered. She went on to say the dressmaker thought they would be there in another week. "Mrs. Rorie said for me to come get the dresses in two weeks. She was sure they would be there and she would be finished by then." Melissa finished setting the table.

Seth sat down and began eating. Melissa was an excellent cook. Or was it that Seth had been eating his own concoctions for too long? Either way, the result was the same. Seth was happy and pleased with his wife and her cooking.

Seth finished eating and said, "I am going back to the toolshed to check out some more of the plows."

He paused as he was going out the door. "We can go to Big Flat any day you want to, just let me know in advance," he said as he closed the door behind him.

He found the single stock plow he wanted for laying off the potato rows and covering the seed after it was planted.

The process of making their first garden was moving forward at a good pace. For several days now, there had been no discussion of the murders and the gossip about them. Seth was enjoying not being asked any questions.

CHAPTER 17

Seth was sitting in a straight-backed chair slicing seed potatoes into four pieces. Melissa instructed him on how to cut up potatoes for planting.

"Make sure there is an equal amount of eyes on each half of the potato, then cut it in half. Next, make sure the half potato has at least one eye on each piece when you cut it into pieces," Melissa said. The instructions sounded complicated to Seth.

Seth was cutting up the smaller red potatoes. Melissa was cutting up the larger white potatoes. When they got home from church the Sunday after Seth plowed the garden for planting, they found two sacks of seed potatoes, one on each side of the front door. It was Wednesday afternoon. They asked everyone they saw who left the seed potatoes.

No one admitted to leaving them. Melissa just shrugged her shoulders and said, "They think they have to look after us."

She was referring to everybody in the community. Seth could not believe the things folks around Cozy had done for them since they got married.

Melissa was cutting up three potatoes and placing them in the basket ready to plant, while Seth was trying to figure out how to cut up one. She laughed continuously as she watched his frustration.

He didn't explain that where he came from in Kentucky, gardening was women's work, especially the planting. He loved doing things with her. They usually ended up having a conversation about things he was learning about the people in the area.

"Daddy's still mad at Uncle Alan for leaving for Oklahoma before Uncle Coy's funeral," Melissa said.

Seth had never met her uncle Alan. He lived several miles away on Tomahawk Creek. It was northwest of where the three brothers were raised on Buffalo River. He was married to a woman from closer to Yellville. Seth did not know anything about the Bryant family before he met Melissa. He met Coy when he was looking for a piece of land. He had only gone to church at Cozy twice before the murder.

Seth listened while Melissa went into a

continuous dialogue about how badly Alan got along with Coy.

"It started when Uncle Alan came back from the army. He was in the war for about Eighteen months, and went to Europe" Melissa said.

She stopped the description of their relationship with a comment.

"I don't know what it's about, I just know when Mama and Daddy would talk about it, they would whisper so us kids couldn't hear," she said, and didn't say anything else about the subject.

She had finished cutting up the white potatoes. They were ready to plant.

"Move your sack over here where I can reach some potatoes, and I'll help you finish yours," she added.

Seth was glad to move the sack. She would have to figure out where the little dots she called eyes were on the red potatoes. The white potatoes' eyes were large. The eyes on the red ones were nothing more than a little black dimple, but he was not going to make an excuse for not being able to keep up with his part of the work.

They finished the potatoes, and they were in separate baskets, ready for planting.

Seth enjoyed planting the potatoes. Melissa had dropped them in the rows, but she complained that the rows were not deep enough. Seth did not know. He thought back to when the potatoes were planted in Kentucky. He believed he was always working on the fence or something else. Melissa instructed him to clean out the last stable, where the goats were kept in the barn, before they bought the place.

He hated cleaning out the stable. He carried the combination of whatever it was in the stable in buckets and spread it over the potatoes after Melissa dropped them in the row. He was relieved when she told him to cover the potatoes by plowing along on each side and creating a ridge over the potato seed. When he got through and put the mule in the barn, he joined Melissa in the house.

"You're experienced now in potato planting. You may not need my help next year when it's time to plant," Melissa said with a laugh, and then began setting the table for supper.

Seth washed up and was getting ready to eat. He came in and sat down in a chair away from the table. She did not like him sitting at the table while she finished getting supper ready.

"Can we take a break from the garden and go to Big Flat tomorrow to get my dresses?" she asked.

Seth knew it was a suggestion more than a question. He agreed quickly by nodding his head, and he wanted to tell her how glad he would be to get out of the dirt for a day. It was going to take some time for him to learn to be a gardener. He would be a good one, though, because he liked to do anything Melissa wanted to do.

CHAPTER 18

It was a warm day for March. There wasn't much wind and the trip to Big Flat was a lot easier than before. Driving the buggy depended on the driver knowing which side of the road was smoothest, plus being able to slow down at the right times. Seth and Melissa had enjoyed visiting during their trip.

There was hardly anyone in Big Flat. Friday's crowd would arrive later in the day. Seth stopped in front of the dress shop and Melissa went in.

"I'm going to see if Preacher Ed can cut my hair," Seth said as he pulled away in the buggy.

There was no one in the barbershop area of the general store. It was usually busy, Seth was surprised. He looked for Preacher Ed and found him in the office area working on the books. He hadn't known that in addition to cutting hair, the preacher also was Jim Rhodes's bookkeeper. Seth started to go to the hardware section when

Preacher Ed stopped him.

"What are you doing today, Seth?" Preacher Ed asked.

"I brought Melissa to pick up the dresses Mrs. Rorie has been making for her," he answered.

Before Seth could ask about a haircut, the preacher looked directly at his hair and asked, "You want me to cut your hair while you wait for her?"

Seth was sitting in the barber chair waiting for Preacher Ed to start cutting his hair before there was anything else said. The preacher walked around and was facing Seth as if he was trying to plan for the haircut.

"You were questioned by the sheriff about the killings," Preacher Ed stated.

There was no hint of it being a question. Seth wondered where the preacher heard about the visit on the ledge by the Searcy County Sheriff.

"I was over at Willie's visiting with him, and we were discussing what happened," Ed added.

The preacher went on to describe his discussion with Willie, the moonshiner. "Willie thinks Sister Rhodes getting killed was not the shooter's plan. While we never got off the wagon seat and went into the barn, Willie has gotten a good description from all the people he's talked to since the shooting.

"Evidently, the shots from the shotgun which killed her went right over Coy's left shoulder. The shot hit her in the neck, underneath her chin." Ed was cutting hair, and he stopped and moved around in front of Seth. They were the only two people in the store. He went on to describe his and Willie's theory that Coy jumped up, pulling sister Rhodes into a sitting position before he was shot in the back. Seth listened and wondered why Preacher Ed was giving him all the details about the bodies.

He went back to cutting hair and didn't say anything else about the incident at the barn. He asked several questions about the people around Cozy and if the discussions had stopped.

Seth was cautious and didn't quote anybody or answer any questions directly. He had learned since the murders that gossip was exchanged either at Willie's barn or in the barbershop where he was sitting. He did not want to make a comment that would bring Sheriff Carson back to see him

He went to see if Melissa was finished with the fitting of her new dresses. She was.

They started the trip back to Cozy. Melissa was talking nonstop about getting the dresses and the discussions with Mrs. Rorie. None of it was anything of interest to Seth. His habit of answering her with an occasional "Yes" and "I know", was coming in handy.

"Do you think our baby will have red hair?" Melissa interrupted her chatter with the question.

Seth jerked the reins so hard when he heard that, the horse almost ran the buggy into the ditch. He stopped the buggy, looked directly at Melissa, dropped the reins, and gave her a big hug.

For the next few minutes, it was a combination of laughter and questions from Seth about how long she had known she was going to have their baby.

"It better have red hair," he finally answered.

The rest of the buggy ride home was a lot slower, as Seth became really concerned about the bouncing of the buggy. He was beginning to wonder if she should've been working as hard as she did in the garden. They got home and there wasn't much discussion. Seth decided during his haircut that he was going back to see Willie Sitton. His thoughts of the barbershop discussion were almost gone, however, and replaced by the thoughts of becoming a father.

CHAPTER 19

A couple of days later, Seth left early in the morning to go to pick up the garden tools. He hoped Willie had finished sharpening them but he also wanted to hear more about the murder scene he heard described by Preacher Ed.

The excitement of becoming a father did not occur to him until Melissa asked him about the color of the baby's hair. They shared several laughs about the way she chose to give him the news. She would smile and look at him before saying, "It better be red."

He wasn't nearly as interested in garden tools as he was the description Preacher Ed gave of the bodies.

He was seated on one of the blocks of wood next to the poker table. Willie was pacing around the room asking questions about his trip to Big Flat. Seth wondered how often Preacher Ed came to see Willie. It had been less than a week since he got his haircut.

"Preacher Ed told you about the description of the bodies," Willie said, not mentioning Sister Rhodes or Coy Bryant by name.

Seth nodded his head. He wondered why they continually wanted to involve him in the discussions. Everyone knew he could not have seen or known any of the details surrounding the shootings.

"I know that's right, whoever shot Sister Rhodes did not intend to kill her," Willie said without any of the previous conversation tying into that opinion. "It had to be that way, because Coy was shot on his left shoulder and again in the middle of his back." Willie gave the same description Preacher Ed had given while he was cutting Seth's hair.

"There are enough people with a good reason to kill Coy Bryant, that's the reason Sheriff Carson can't get any leads on the shooter." Willie was determined to keep discussing the shooting. "The reason I'm telling you all this is because Melissa's family probably knows something." Willie stopped and sat down on one of the blocks across from Seth. "I know it won't hurt you and Melissa because Haskell Bryant is a good man and her mother is Fred Hudson's first cousin; they're good folks."

Willie interrupted his thoughts about the shooting and Melissa's family.

"I got your tools sharp," he said. "But let me finish telling you about what we figured out from all the things I've heard that happened in the barn." He was referring to himself and Preacher Ed.

He went into the feed room where he kept the 'shine and returned with two tin cups about half-full. It was raw 'shine, not a hot toddy. He handed one of the cups to Seth.

"Sip that slow. If it's too strong I've got some weaker stuff." Willie sat back down and held his cup with both hands in front of his face, looking at Seth before he began the next story about what he believed about the shootings.

"I looked Coy's barn over real good before I built this one," Willie said as he sat the cup down on the poker table and stood up again. He first started to open the door and then looked around at Seth as if he wanted him to follow. He went back and picked up the cup with the 'shine in it. He sat back down.

"There's a little stall on the back corner of this barn, just like the one on Coy's barn," he began his description of the two barns. "They're for keeping a mare before she foals or a cow that's about to have a calf."

Seth was wondering where this story was going. Willie began to explain how he thought the shooter managed to get into the loft undetected. He went on to describe how the shooter got there early and put his horse in that stall on the back corner of the barn.

"There's a ladder in that stall with a trapdoor where you can get up into the loft," Willie continued. "He went in and hid behind the bales of hay and waited for Coy and Sister Rhodes to get there. There is no other way it could've happened."

He completed a description of how the shooter was watching Sister Rhodes and Coy Bryant as they began their lovemaking.

"He stepped out and was standing up over them when he fired the shot that killed Sister Rhodes." Willie said it like he knew it for fact. "He then shot Coy. He was down that ladder in the stall and on his horse and out of there while Carl was getting the mules under control and turning the wagon around."

Willie leaned back against the wall. He looked at Seth. "Me and Preacher Ed have spent a lot of time figuring this out, but we've not said a word to anybody else besides you." Willie stopped with the story.

Seth wondered why he was sharing this with him. All the questions directed toward Seth since the shooting came from people who seemed to be prying, trying to learn something, which Seth could not possibly think of what it was.

They left the barn and went to the shop where Willie showed him the tools. They were in perfect shape. Seth looked at each tool while Willie explained why he put the type of point on each tool. The garden hoe had a slim blade on one side, while the other side was twice as wide and not as sharp.

"That narrow side is for digging deeper into the dirt, the other side is for moving dirt next to the plants" Willie explained. "That's a woman's hoe, and I hope you got a long handle for it."

Seth did not mention Melissa was pregnant. He paid Willie for sharpening the tools, over his objections to being paid.

Seth left the barn with Willie standing and watching as he rode away. Seth was confused about all he had heard. He had wondered for over three months why everyone continued to share something about the murders.

He made it back to Cozy and to his farm before dark.

He would put the handles in the tools tomorrow. He didn't share any of his and Willie's conversation with Melissa. He also didn't share any of Preacher Ed's comments during the haircut. His curiosity was at an all-time high. He believed Willie's description of the murder was right, because it explained how quickly the shooter got on his horse and rode away from the barn.

CHAPTER 20

Seth's thoughts continued to concentrate on his visit with Willie while he was putting the handles back into the tools. He was shimming a couple of the handles, and wondered why they were too small to go back in the tool he removed them from before he took them to Willie for sharpening. He got four handles in before Melissa called him for breakfast.

"Daddy came while you were at Willie's and asked us to go with them to Uncle Alan's in two weeks," she said.

Seth didn't answer. He was covering his biscuits with gravy. He placed two sausage patties on top of the gravy and began eating them with the biscuits and gravy.

"Did you hear what I said?" Melissa asked. Her tone was almost irritable. Seth noticed since she had told him about the baby, her patience was a little shorter.

"Yes, I heard you," he answered after he took a

drink of his coffee.

His mind was racing as he tried to recall all he had heard about Melissa's uncle Alan. There was something remiss about the relationship between the three brothers. Seth was never told any bad things about Melissa's family, and her mother and dad treated him like he was their own.

"Are we going?" he finally asked.

"Yes, I want to go." Melissa refilled his coffee cup. "Uncle Alan and his son, Leon, will be there."

After several seconds—it felt like minutes—Seth asked a question.

"What's different about this visit?" He almost finished eating the biscuits and gravy before Melissa answered.

Seth got up and took the jar of molasses, the jar Willie gave him, and got a spoonful of butter to stir into it. When he started to stir them together, Melissa stopped and was watching him.

"I don't know." She seemed to be trying to think of what caused the tension between the Bryant family members.

Seth thought about all the descriptions Willie gave of Melissa's family. He ended his dialogue about the Bryant family by saying they were cousins. Willie said his grandmother was a sister to Haskell's grandmother. Seth was not surprised. He learned early on when he first arrived on Big Creek that most people in the area were from Wayne County, Tennessee. They all were connected either through marriage or blood relatives. He became cautious about making any remarks. He remembered back home in Eastern Kentucky, that people either had a fight or someone got shot for making a bad remark.

Melissa finally said, "It has something to do with Leon and when he was born." She paused for a minute. "He looks like a member of the Bryant family, but Mama said it caused trouble when he was born."

Melissa started picking up the dirty dishes and putting them in the dishpan to wash. Seth was left wondering what he was hearing and why it was important.

Seth returned to the toolshed and resumed putting the handles in the tools. He was preoccupied with all the conversations over the last several weeks. They seemed to intensify after he went to Big Flat to get the hinges for the corral gate.

He was comfortable visiting with Preacher Ed and Willie, but he also wondered why they continued to want to tell him what they believed about the murders. He was at ease visiting with Willie when he went to pick up the tools at the bridge. He thought about Willie's theory of how the murderer was in the barn when Sister Rhodes and Coy Bryant arrived.

He was curious how he was able to place his horse in the stall in the back corner of the barn and not have him start nickering when the buggy and Coy's horse arrived. He was told when he was a kid, that you could put blinders on a horse and the horse would be quiet. He also had been told you could put a sack over a horse's head and lead it from a burning barn.

He wondered if Sheriff Carson and Willie had discussed the theory about the horse in the stable. He thought about Willie's theory that Sister Rhodes was not the intended victim. He questioned that being the truth. There was no way the shooter could leave a witness. He believed both shots hit their intended victim.

Seth's theory was that she was shot first because the shooter would not have an open shot if he shot Coy first. Seth was irritated at himself. There was every reason for him to stop thinking about something he could not see from over two hundred yards away. He also wondered how long the discussion was going to last.

He finished putting the tools in the rack where he kept them stored. They were ready for the work in the garden.

He left the toolshed and went to the garden and inspected the potato rows. "As soon as we see any sign they are coming up, we have to knock down the ridges," Melissa had said when they'd planted them.

Seth believed it was time to do that. He could see several areas where the dirt showed signs of movement from underneath. He went to the house and asked Melissa to come to the garden. He needed her to show him what needed to be done.

Seth felt a little inadequate trying to make a garden when his experience was limited to the few plants he had grown next to his cabin on the ledge.

The ridges were nice and flat on all the potato rows. Seth followed Melissa's instructions. Using the hoe Willie said was a woman's hoe, he had flattened the ridges to about six inches in width. He was lucky and did not damage any of the plants. When he looked back after he was finished, he could see several potato plants coming through the dirt. They were just waiting for him to uncover them.

Seth enjoyed uncovering the potatoes and flattening the ridges of each row. It gave him a mental break from thinking about all the questions he was being asked about things, which he had no idea how to answer.

CHAPTER 21

Seth and Melissa's buggy was third in line behind Fred Hudson's. Seth wasn't aware that the trip to Melissa's uncle Alan Bryant was going to be a caravan of buggies from around Cozy. Fred and his family got to Seth and Melissa's house before they were ready to go.

Seth was making his first trip ever up the south side of Buffalo River. For the most part they traveled along the ridges above the river and made three trips down different hollows to the riverbanks. They were now following Tomahawk Creek upstream to Melissa's uncle Alan's farm.

Seth was impressed with the good farmland where the creek suddenly became a smaller stream after passing two large springs. They eventually followed one of the spring branches to a large plantation-style farmhouse. Melissa commented that her grandfather gave Uncle Alan the best farm he owned.

They were passing fields of corn and some fields of alfalfa. The hill land above the fields was pasture. Seth didn't understand how Melissa's uncle could be working in the oil fields of Oklahoma when he had a large farming operation.

They parked their buggy beside Melissa's parents' buggy. Seth tied their horse to the hitching rail and returned to help Melissa down from the buggy. He wasn't sure she had shared their news about the baby with anyone.

The first thirty minutes was taken up with introductions. Seth immediately liked Melissa's Uncle Alan. He followed him to the large veranda across the front of the house. He had seen a couple of houses around Leslie identical to this one. They sat visiting and Seth did not enter into any of the conversation.

Mostly the conversations were about Alan's work in Oklahoma. The 1930s were a conflicted economic time. The Depression was terrible in some cities, but the farmland of northern Arkansas and the oil fields of Oklahoma seemed to be untouched.

The visiting moved from the veranda to the backyard. Again, Seth was surprised when he saw a row of picnic tables underneath an area covered by a roof. He followed Fred Hudson and Melissa's dad to a table being set for the men. It was his first time to ever be at a gathering this large.

"Let us pray." Alan Bryant's voice rang loudly over the area and the people seated at the tables.

Seth listened to the prayer and was amazed by the sound of his voice and the rhythm he was speaking. It was very close to Preacher Ed's voice. He wondered if Melissa's uncle Alan was ever a preacher.

Seth looked at the table where the women were seated when he heard loud laughter. Melissa was getting a lot of attention. She was finished telling the women they were expecting the baby. She was telling the story about their discussion of the baby's hair.

"It better be red," was repeated by several of the women eating at the table with Melissa, followed by laughter.

Seth received congratulations from all the men. The food was fantastic. They were served by two colored people. Seth learned they were descendants of the slaves the Bryant's brought with them from Wayne County Tennessee. They were no longer in servitude, but chose to stay with the Bryant family and work for them. When Melissa's grandfather moved to Tomahawk Creek from Buffalo River, they moved with him. The family was several generations removed from the original slaves.

Seth never asked any questions as he was being told about the history of the farm at Tomahawk and the Bryant family. They finished the meal. Alan Bryant moved over and shook Seth's hand a second time and turned and introduced him to Leon Bryant.

He did not refer to him as his son. Seth thought nothing of it at the time.

"Seth, do you want to go look at the livestock?" he asked.

Seth followed him to the corral. It was full of Hereford cattle. They were obviously of a good bloodline. The tour continued and he barely tolerated the smell of the hog barn. He was pleased when they went across a small field to the horse corral.

There were several saddle-bred horses, and there were three work mares heavy with foals. Fred Hudson asked several questions about the horses. Seth listened as Melissa's Uncle Alan answered his questions.

"Can I see your studs?" Fred asked.

Seth noticed the hesitation expressed on Alan Bryant's face before he answered.

"I hate to bother them," Alan Bryant answered as he started toward the stables.

He opened the stable doors and let out three horses. Seth hoped no one saw his expression. He believed he was looking at the chestnut-colored horse with the black mane he saw climbing the mountain away from the barn the day Coy Bryant was killed.

Seth regained his composure without saying a word. He turned and kicked at a clump of hay outside the corral. He kicked it again until it went back under the corral fence. The horse that put him in shock came over and ate the hay. He looked at it closer and confirmed what he thought when the horse tossed its head after eating the hay.

The tour of the farm was finished. The men returned to the veranda where they sat earlier. The rest of the visit was spent either bantering about how much someone had changed over the years or reminiscing about things they did as boys. Coy Bryant was never mentioned once during the visit. Fred Hudson sat next to Seth after they got back to the veranda. He would comment and laugh when he was spoken to. He never asked a question.

Haskell Bryant, Melissa's dad, seemed nervous at the time they arrived and still seemed to be nervous. Seth wondered about that also.

Hours later, they were in their buggies and on their way back to Cozy. The goodbyes and the invitations while they were leaving took about as long as it did to eat the meal. Melissa sat quietly during the first few minutes they were back in their buggy.

"Did you enjoy meeting my family?" she asked Seth.

He looked down the reins to the back of the horse's head pulling the buggy. He thought about all the questions which raced through his mind after seeing the chestnut-colored horse. He decided to listen to Melissa and ignore his suspicions.

Finally, he said, "I enjoyed meeting them, and they were all nice to me."

Melissa was chattering continuously about all the things her relatives said to her about the baby.

Seth drove the buggy, half-listening to her, with the other half trying to figure out what he learned.

CHAPTER 22

Seth finished laying off more rows in the garden. Melissa wanted to plant some beans, squash, and a couple of more vegetables. He enjoyed plowing with the little brown mule. He walked steadily and straight, making it easy to lay off a good row for planting.

He put the plow in the toolshed after he took the harness off the mule and put him in the stable. He fed the mule four ears of corn. He remembered feeding his other mule twice that much. It was a lot easier taking care of this one.

He was still having trouble concentrating on his work after seeing the chestnut-colored horse in Melissa's Uncle Alan's corral. Melissa's chatter during the trip home didn't perk his interest until she said, "Did I tell you what Mama told me about Leon?"

Seth didn't answer, but she continued. "The day before we went over there, she told me it was time to tell me the secret behind the way Uncle Alan felt about Uncle Coy."

Seth listened intently for the rest of the buggy trip home. Melissa told him about Leon being born four months after her Uncle Alan got home from the Army. He went to Germany during the big war and was over there for almost a year before he came home.

Seth's opinion about Melissa's Uncle Coy was good before Melissa started sharing this story. She told how Alan took care of his farm and let Coy have some stock cattle from the original herd given to him by their dad before he went to the Army.

"Grandpa Bryant gave practically everything he owned to Alan because he was the oldest son. It never bothered my dad." She paused for a second and added, "He expected it to be that way. Mama said Uncle Alan would not divorce Aunt Mary over her having Leon. He accepted Leon as his son, but he never spoke to his brother again."

Melissa stopped talking about the family dispute. Seth was stuck in his mind trying to figure how it was possible that one of Melissa's uncles shot the other one.

He knew Haskell Bryant, his father-in-law, never went to church until after the shooting in the barn. He knew Fred Hudson got along well with Haskell. He never knew anything about either one of their relationships with Coy.

Seth got the bean seeds and started dropping them in the rows Melissa said she wanted planted with beans. He wondered what kind of beans he was planting. The seed was bigger than any beans he'd ever seen. She showed him a set of poles in the attic of the toolshed. She said those would have to be set up for the beans to grow on. Seth remembered seeing that back in Kentucky on a neighbor's farm. His folks had grown their beans next to the fence at the lower edge of the garden, and his mother made sure the plants went up the fence.

He planted a short row of squash and finished it out with cucumbers. He wasn't sure if he was cut out to be a gardener. He was enjoying it, but only because of Melissa.

Seth decided he was going back to see Willie. He didn't know when he could go, but he wanted to listen to Willie tell more stories about the Bryant family. Seth knew there was no way he could ever mention what he thought when he saw the chestnut-colored horse with the black mane in Alan Bryant's corral.

Seth watched the sunset. He watched the shadow of the barn lengthen until it extended across the garden. The potatoes, not in the shadow, were glistening in the evening sun. He had strained the milk after he milked the cow and filled two jugs with it. He carried those to the spring box and brought back one cold one for supper. Life was good. But his mind was trying to sort through what he knew for sure and what was just his suspicions.

He made plans to go see Willie. He was trying

to think of an excuse this time. He decided he needed to get the wing plow for plowing the potatoes sharpened. He found it sticking between two logs. He had no idea what it was for until Melissa told him it was for plowing potatoes and making sure there was enough dirt around the plants to keep the potatoes covered when they started to grow.

CHAPTER 23

Willie was in the blacksmith shop cranking the bellows. Seth tied his horse to the hitching rail. He took the wing plow from the sack behind the saddle. He took it out of the sack as he walked into Willie's blacksmith shop.

"What have you got there?" Willie asked after he stopped cranking the bellows.

He had not greeted Seth with any of their usual greetings. It was his style to work until someone got close enough to hear him. Most people in the area were the same way. When Seth arrived years earlier, he wasn't used to people not greeting each other with a "hello".

He was used to it now. He laid the plow on the work stand beside the forage.

Willie looked at it. "I made that for Paul Avey," Willie said as he picked it up. "There is supposed to be a smaller one, too."

Willie turned and faced Seth.

"What do you want me to do to it?" Willie asked. Seth picked the plow point back up.

"Don't it need to be sharp?" he asked.

"No, it goes behind the bull-tongue," Willie said, referring to the plow point already on the single stock.

Willie went on to explain how the wing plow went behind the other plow point. He also told Seth he made two different sizes and they were to be used together, with both of them fastened to the plow behind the bull-togue, the main point. Seth stood there, confused. He would have to ask Melissa how this worked.

He was embarrassed as he put the wing plow back in the sack and took it to his horse.

"Don't run off, let's visit a while." Willie left the shop. Seth followed him to the barn.

Without asking if Seth wanted a toddy, Willie began heating water. He stirred some sugar into the water as it got warm.

Steam was coming from the water when the door to the barn opened. It was Preacher Ed. He shook hands with Seth.

Willie continued stirring the water and sugar as it came to a boil. He took three tin cups down from their hooks. They were hanging on a series of nails driven into a log beside the door of the corn crib. There were also a couple of other items, including a small brush with a long handle, hanging beside the cups.

Seth sat down across the room, away from the stove. Willie was watching the water as it came to a boil. Preacher Ed sat down across from Seth on his right. Willie sat a cup on the poker table in front of both of them. He took a jar of 'shine from the shelf and started pouring it into the water while it was boiling. He then poured a portion of the liquid into the cups on the table. He poured the last of the toddy into his cup and sat down.

Seth didn't touch the cup in front of him. Preacher Ed looked at Seth with no expression and picked up the cup closest to him. Seth picked up the cup Willie had set in front of him. Willie stood, sipping on his toddy as he watched the preacher and Seth hesitating about taking a drink.

Simultaneously, Preacher Ed and Seth started drinking the mixture of moonshine, water, and sugar. There was no conversation until after they both began sipping from the cups.

"You went to the Bryant reunion?" Willie directed the question to Seth. Before Seth could answer, Willie continued.

"Them was big events until Alan Bryant came home from the Army years ago," Willie said.

Willie finally sat down. Preacher Ed was nervous. Seth watched the preacher's eyes while Willie poured the toddies into the cups. It was obvious he was going to take a drink. Seth wondered about the stories he heard about Preacher Ed and Willie. He was getting a firsthand look at their friendship.

"My mother was a first cousin to the Bryant boys' dad." Willie looked at Seth and added, "We never missed one of the reunions until they quit having them."

Willie went on with the story of how bad the relationship became between Alan and Coy. He described how vicious the gossip was about Coy and Alan's wife. He told Seth things Seth already knew. He had guessed about why the relationship went bad between the two brothers after Leon Bryant was born only four months after Alan returned from the Army.

Seth was wondering why Willie was choosing to tell him the stories. He knew Willie had a purpose for telling the story. After he told the story about Alan's hatred for Coy, he looked at Preacher Ed.

"Should I tell Seth the gossip about people thinking Alan did the shooting?" He directed the question to the preacher.

Preacher Ed was embarrassed and uncomfortable. He had promised himself never to drink again after the embarrassment of getting drunk. He was breaking that promise to himself.

"Willie, we know Seth is married to Melissa. We know her mother is Fred Hudson's cousin. We know Haskell Bryant is a fine man, but he never came to church at Cozy until after Coy was shot." The preacher sat the cup with about half of the contents left in it back on the table. He stood up, walked around the table, and looked back at Seth.

"We've wondered, Seth, why you never came

around much before the shooting." Preacher Ed went back around the table and picked up the cup he had been drinking from. "Me and Willie have a different relationship than anyone else I know." The preacher smiled for the first time since he arrived at the barn. "Willie knows more about people than I will ever know." The preacher made that remark as a statement of fact.

He went on to explain how peoples' attitudes change around him. He talked about how Willie always just treated him like a friend. He began to explain how Fred Hudson and Willie were the two best friends he made after coming to Big Flat. He spent a lot of time giving background information to Seth on what he believed caused Coy to be shot.

Finally, Willie interrupted. "What the preacher's trying to get around to saying is, a lot of people think Alan Bryant has to be the shooter."

Seth sat in shock. He could not believe what he was hearing, and under no circumstances was he prepared to make any comment.

Willie began to explain how impossible it would be for Alan Bryant, living over twenty miles away, to show up in Coy's barn at the right time to be waiting for him to meet Sister Rhodes.

"Somebody else would have to tell him when to be there, and that would be next to impossible."

Seth still had not made his first comment.

"Ellen heard," Willie referred to his wife. "You and Melissa are having a baby?" There was a questioning tone in Willie's statement.

"Yes, we're having a kid." Seth smiled and relaxed when he gave the answer, hoping the subject was about to change.

CHAPTER 24

Seth fastened the bull tongue in front of the two wing plows on the single stock. He did not ask Melissa how to do it. He was embarrassed about having to ask her when he didn't know something about gardening.

He caught the mule and was harnessing him to the plow. It was a beautiful morning, but his thoughts continued to return to the conversations with Willie and Preacher Ed.

After the discussion of his and Melissa's baby, Preacher Ed commented about how disruptive all the accusations and talk about the shootings had become.

"It doesn't matter who I am visiting with, they eventually ask me questions about any progress being made on who did the shooting," the preacher said. "I don't have any answers, and do not believe the sheriff of Searcy County will ever find the answers," he continued. He looked at Willie and added, "I just wish we hadn't gone down there, Willie."

Willie stood and walked around in front of Seth. Seth tried to remember exactly how he answered Preacher Ed.

"We both have too much contact with too many people to avoid the discussions," was Willie's comment.

Seth was amazed at how many questions entered his mind since the day he sat on the bluff watching the activity at the barn. Regardless of what he was doing, his mind eventually went back to that day.

Melissa yelled for him to come to breakfast.

"You did a good job plowing the potatoes," Melissa said as Seth came to the table. He had spent several minutes washing his hands and getting the dust off before he came in to eat. She did not mention his trip to Willie's barn. If she knew, he took the big wing plow to be sharpened and didn't realize it did not need sharpening. Seth appreciated Willie not lecturing him about not knowing how the wing plow worked. Seth was getting along with everyone while he learned to be a farmer.

Melissa placed a plate of scrambled eggs between them to share. There were the usual biscuits along with Seth's favorite, chocolate gravy. He never heard of chocolate gravy until he married Melissa. The Bryant and Hudson families cooked a lot of things Seth had never eaten before.

Seth ate in silence. He appreciated Melissa not questioning him about Willie, and he was not going to tell her about seeing Preacher Ed.

He was not bothered by Preacher Ed sharing the toddy with him and Willie. He liked the honesty and relaxed conversation they had. His thoughts ever since yesterday were cluttered with him trying to reconcile what he saw from the bluff, what he heard since the sheriff came, and questioned him along with seeing the horse at Melissa's uncle Alan's corral.

He was sure it had been the horse he saw climbing the hill away from Big Creek the day of the shooting. He added the horse to his thoughts, along with all the things Preacher Ed and Willie brought up during their discussion at the barn.

He finished eating and took his coffee and went to the east side of the house to sit on the porch. It was getting hot for the middle of June. Melissa joined him.

"Mama and Daddy came by yesterday while you were gone." She had not told him until now. Seth waited to see if she was going to tell him anything about their visit.

"Mama said I was lucky to not have morning sickness," Melissa said. After a minute she added, "Mama said she could not eat a bite for the first four months when she got pregnant with me."

Seth wondered how much of that could be true. How could a woman stay alive and the baby develop without any nourishment? He made some comments but did not add to the conversation while he listened to Melissa. He was preoccupied trying to figure out everything he had heard since the shooting. His visit with Willie and Preacher Ed just added to the confusion of his thoughts.

CHAPTER 25

Seth finished out the day working in the garden. He weeded all the vegetables that were coming up. He was tired when he went to bed and had eaten his supper in silence. Melissa came to bed sometime later but did not wake him.

He got up early the next morning. When it came daylight, he was riding east toward Big Creek. He was going back to the place he sold on the ledge. He wanted to see how much he could've seen from the rock where he sat and try to reconcile it with all the gossip he had heard since the shootings.

He didn't wake Melissa, but left her a note to tell her that he would be gone most of the day. "I'm going looking for some things I may have left at the old place," it said. He never found a couple of splitting wedges after he moved, and believed he left them sticking between the logs next to the bluff. It was the reason he gave to himself for going back to the ledge.

He made good time. When he got on the trail leading to his old cabin, he wondered why it did not appear to have been traveled for quite some time. The closer he got, the more he realized there was no sign of anyone being around for a while. He never heard anyone say anything about the fellow leaving who bought the place.

He was gone. The door was standing about half-open when Seth stopped. He tied the horse where he always tied his mule. When he looked at the sod roof, there were persimmon sprouts growing up out of the sod. The fellow he sold it to did not let the goat keep the roof clean. He looked inside and the wood stove was gone. Seth was startled by a skunk that ran out the door as he started in. He was proud the skunk chose not to spray him with its stench.

He went around the cabin to look for the wedges where he thought he had left them. The spring was dry. Seth lived there several years before he met Melissa. Seth wondered why the spring had gone dry. That would be a good reason for the property to be deserted. There was no other water within a half-mile, besides Big Creek below the bluff.

Seth continued to look around and could not believe how fast the weeds and briars were taking over the area of the cabin. He remembered seeing deserted property before, but usually it didn't grow up with underbrush as fast as this. He knew the new owner had been living there in January.

He found the wedges. They were not as rusty as he expected. He put them in the saddlebags and led the horse through the woods toward the bluff. The trail where he skidded logs to make handles was still clear of weeds and grass. He wondered why it wasn't grown up like all the other areas around the cabin.

He tied the horse up and walked out to the rock. He sat down and began to look at the barn. The corn was growing as usual in the field between the bluff and the barn. It was beginning to tassel, and Seth could see the silks coming out of the ears growing on the stalks.

After looking at the cornfield and thinking how well he could see corn growing, he wondered why he couldn't remember more details from the day of the murder. One reason he wanted to come back to the bluff was to see how much of his memory was distorted. The corn was growing a lot closer than the barn. It was immediately below the bluff, but as he looked farther toward the barn, he could not see well enough to tell if there were any tassels or corn silk growing out of the new ears developing on the stalks.

There were two horses in the corral next to the barn, and there were some steers in the big corral above the barn. Somebody was farming the field and using the barn as usual. Seth did not know who was taking over Coy Bryant's property.

He spent several minutes trying to visualize the order of the things that had happened the day of the shooting. There were crows in the trees just like the day of the shooting. They were trying to feed on the cornfield. They were making a lot of noise between their trips to and from the field.

He remembered the interruption of the noise by the shotgun blast. He remembered watching the wagon as it went toward the barn. He remembered watching the mules trying to run back with the wagon the same direction they came from. He stopped thinking for a minute and looked back toward the cabin. He tried to remember how many trips he made to and from the cabin during the day of the shooting. He couldn't remember.

Finally, he stood up on the rock and looked toward the hill where he was sure he had seen Alan Bryant's horse climbing the hill. He could not see well enough through the brush from the rock to see what he remembered. He went to the gap where he believed he was standing when he saw the horse. He couldn't remember why he had moved from the rock to where he was now, but as he looked toward the trail climbing the hill, he could clearly see a gap about fifty yards wide and clear enough for him to have seen the horse as he remembered it.

Seth mounted his horse and rode away from the ledge. The trip had satisfied his curiosity about his memories. He was sure the horse he saw at Melissa's uncle's was the horse climbing the hill.

He was in no hurry to get home. He rode very slowly as he tried to decide what he should do. He made it home in the mid-afternoon.

CHAPTER 26

"Did you find the wedges at the cabin?" Melissa asked. Seth heard the question but was lost in thought about the time spent on the ledge trying to remember the events at the barn the day of the shooting. He finally realized what her question was.

"Yes, they were right where I left them," he answered, and then added, "The place was deserted. The man that bought it is gone."

He went on to tell her about the spring being dry and no furnishings of any kind left in the cabin. She asked several questions about the man Seth sold it to.

"Why would he buy the land and then desert it?" She said more of a statement than a question.

Seth answered that he didn't know and went back to check on the horse to see if he needed more feed. He went by the garden on his way back to the house. He was not going to do any garden work today.

He spent the rest of the afternoon reconciling his memory with the gossip since the shootings. He came to a conclusion. He was as sure as he could be that the horse in Melissa's uncle Alan Bryant's corral was the one he saw leaving the shooting.

He knew he wasn't going to say a word about it. All the things Willie and Preacher Ed said while he was at the barn were questions he couldn't answer about the horse. How could Alan Bryant have known when to come to the barn? There were no answers to any of the questions. He could not give a description of the man riding the horse.

When he thought back over the last six months, he knew what he witnessed at the barn changed his life. He went to Cozy to hear the talk about the shooting. He met Melissa while he was there. It was love at first sight. He was happy with her and all they accomplished in such a short period of time. He was acquainted with Preacher Ed and respected him very much. He would never betray the preacher's trust, and was not bothered by the preacher sharing the toddy with him and Willie. He knew Willie was the center of influence in the whole area.

If he chose to tell the sheriff what he knew, he was sure it would raise more questions than could be answered. He had listened to the sheriff's comment as he stood on the rock and looked toward the trail where the horse went up the hill away from the creek. When he stood on the rock and looked toward the trail, he agreed with the sheriff that there was no way he could've seen through the tree limbs. He was not going to take the sheriff back to the ledge and show him where he was standing when he saw the horse and rider go up the hill.

There was too much to be lost by speaking up. Melissa's family knew about Alan Bryant's feelings toward his brother Coy. There was no explanation for why he would raise a child fathered by his brother while he was in the Army. Seth didn't know whether that was true or not. But he agreed with Preacher Ed and Willie that it wasn't believable Alan would wait eighteen years and suddenly decide to kill Coy.

Seth made a vow in his mind. It was settled. He would never take part in another discussion with anyone about the shootings. He never wanted to give any hint about his thoughts when he saw the horse in Alan Bryant's corral. He would keep his vow of silence. He was in a good situation. He had a farm and a wife expecting a child. They were members of a family respected in the community.

Coy Bryant's and Sister Rhode's deaths would just be part of the history along Big Creek. She would be remembered in Big Flat, and Coy would be remembered throughout the area, mostly as a religious man with a weakness for women.

Melissa prepared another good supper. Seth was

able to join in with her chatter as she talked about all of her plans for the new baby.

"If it's a boy, what do you want to name him?" she asked. Seth's mind raced, as he had not given it any thought before.

"I like William Frederick." Seth had no idea where that name came from or why it just popped out of his mouth.

Melissa started laughing. "I like the name, but I'm afraid people would call him 'Billy Fred'." she said.

Seth joined her in laughter. Melissa laughed until tears ran down her cheeks. Neither one of them knew why her calling him Billy Fred seemed so funny.

They finished supper and went to the porch. A new day was beginning at the Tabor household. They were moving forward, and hopefully Seth could bury what he knew somewhere in his memory.

It was a beautiful July sunset in Cozy Home, Arkansas.

ABOUT THE AUTHOR

Sam Pemberton was born on Bratton Creek, at an old homestead that hadn't changed much since the pioneer days. The year was 1944. Pemberton graduated from Big Flat high school. After their graduation in 1962, Sam married the love of his life, Patricia Treat.

He has worked construction in the drywall trade for most of his life. Sam presently lives in the beautiful Ozarks and continues in construction. He loves writing his stories and enjoys his morning coffee and porch time.

OTHER BOOKS BY SAM PEMBERTON

The Moonshiner and the Preacher
Finding Big Flat
Zeek's Journey to Freedom
Missy's Life as a Slave
Livin' Under Goldies Rule

Made in the USA
Coppell, TX
14 December 2023

26130899R00066